IRISH LEGENDS

NEWGRANGE, TARA & THE BOYNE VALLEY

EITHNE MASSEY
ILLUSTRATED BY LISA JACKSON

THE O'BRIEN PRESS
DUBLIN

Eithne Massey is the author of the bestselling *Best-Loved Irish Legends*, retellings of Irish myths for young children, which has been published in English, French and German. In 2015 Eithne was joint winner of the Literacy Association of Ireland Special Merit Award for her historical children's novel, *Blood Brother, Swan Sister*, set at the time of the Battle of Clontarf. Her other children's novels that blend history and fantasy include *The Silver Stag of Bunratty* and *Where the Stones Sing*. Her adaptation of the award-winning animated movie *The Secret of Kells* is set in the time of the early Viking raids.

Lisa Jackson is a Dublin-based illustrator, painter and comic-book colourist and letterist. Her books for children include the hugely popular *Best-Loved Irish Legends*, and also for The O'Brien Press: *The Henny Penny Tree* and *Ice Dreams*.

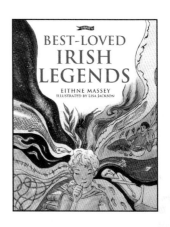

Praise for
Best-Loved Irish Legends

'A book to keep and treasure'
Irish Examiner

'Perfect for storytime'
Irish American Magazine

'A collection of old favourites, including "The Children of Lir"
and "The Salmon of Knowledge"
in one handsomely illustrated volume for 4+'
Irish Independent

CONTENTS

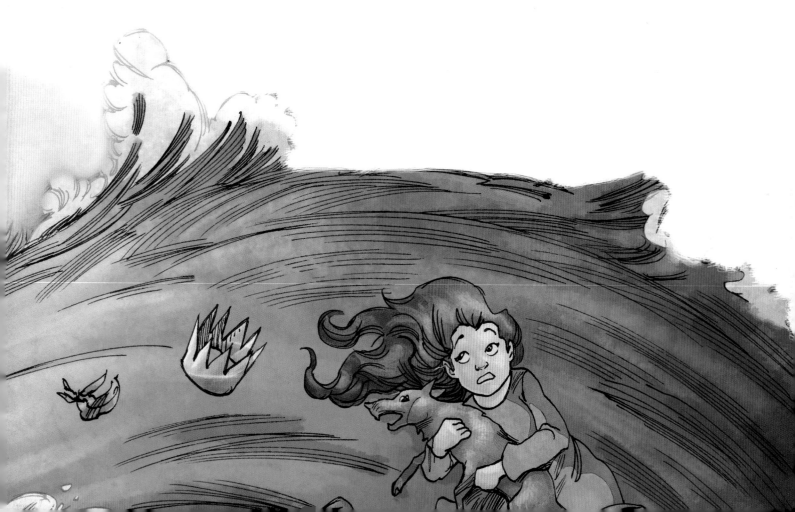

HOW THE BOYNE WAS BORN

⊠　⊠　⊠

This is a story about a princess. It is also a story about a well. The well was called the Well of Wisdom. Nuts fell from the nine magic hazel trees that grew over it. The nuts contained all the knowledge in the world. A salmon swam in the well and swallowed the nuts. But no one was allowed to look into its dark depths but Nechtan, the greatest magician in the land.

He was a king, and he was also the chief of the druids who guarded the Well of Wisdom.

PRONUNCIATION GUIDE:

Bóann: *bowann;* **Nechtan:** *necktann*

And the princess? Her name was Bóann. Although she lived in a beautiful palace, she was a very bored princess. She wasn't allowed to run or jump. She was supposed to sit quietly and not ask any questions. She spent every day sitting and sewing with her ladies-in-waiting. Whenever she asked a question they said, 'Princesses don't need to know that.'

But Bóann wanted to know about the places beyond the palace walls. She wanted to see the sea and the mountains, the fields and woods, and meet lots of people.

One day Bóann was feeling especially bored. She walked restlessly round and round in her room. Her one friend in the whole palace, her dog, Dabilla, watched from her cushion. Bóann told Dabilla everything.

Now she plucked her little dog up from her cushion and whispered, 'We are going to visit the Well of Wisdom.'

Dabilla barked sharply. She knew that Bóann was not supposed to go near that well.

Bóann held Dabilla up so she could look into her eyes. 'You don't think it's a good idea, do you?' she said.

Dabilla barked sharply again.

She kept barking as Bóann carried her to the grove of hazels. She barked even louder when Bóann lifted the heavy wooden cover of the well. She pawed at Bóann frantically when the princess looked down into the water.

It was the darkest and the deepest well in the world. For a moment, as Bóann looked in, there was a great stillness. She could see her own face peering back at her from the depths.

Then, there was a flash of silver fin. A rushing movement. The water swirled. As Bóann watched, all the knowledge in the well rose towards her in a dark green wave. The water kept rising higher and higher. Dabilla was barking madly now.

Bóann shivered. She tried to push the wooden cover back over the well. But it was too late, because the water was pouring over the edge! The rushing wave knocked her off her feet. She just had time to clasp Dabilla in her arms before she was swept away.

Nechtan and the druids ran towards the well. They looked on in horror as the water carried Bóann along. She was battered against trees and rocks. She clutched Dabilla harder to her. She wasn't bored now. She was terrified.

The wild waters carried her past the palace. She saw her ladies, their mouths open in horror.

The ladies dropped their sewing and started to scream, but Bóann could not hear them. Her ears were full of rushing water. Her mind was filling up with all the knowledge of the world.

'Goodbye!' she called to the ladies. 'No more sewing!'

And now she was no longer scared.

Mile after mile, further and further the water travelled, moving faster and faster, curving around mountains, cutting through plains, carrying everything with it. Bóann saw hills and houses and the wonderful world outside her palace walls.

'Hello, world!' she called.

Now the sea was ahead of her, the mighty kingdom of Manannán Mac Lir. She could see his sea horses galloping towards her, their white manes streaming over the crests of the waves.

'Hello, sea!' called Bóann.

Bóann realised that the water was not carrying her any longer. She *was* the water. Inside her was the knowledge she had looked for. And she was inside the flow of the knowledge.

She was Bóann, the river.

The river Bóann.

The river Boyne.

Bóann had become the goddess of the river. Her voice was the river's voice.

And what of her little dog? Faithful Dabilla became a rock on the seashore, just where Bóann runs into the ocean. She is so happy to be close by her mistress forever. You can see her still.

FIONN'S FIRST ADVENTURES

❖   ❖   ❖

Fionn was a young boy who lived on the banks of the Boyne river. He was the servant of a man called Finnegas. Fionn had to do all the work: the cooking, the cleaning, gathering firewood and lighting the fires. But the one thing he was not allowed to do was fish.

His master, Finnegas, spent all *his* days fishing in the part of the river where a huge salmon lived.

One day Fionn heard a cry of joy. Finnegas was pulling the biggest salmon Fionn had ever seen out of the river! The salmon winked at Fionn.

'Cook this!' called Finnegas, his voice shaking with excitement. 'But be sure that you don't eat any of it, not even a bit of its skin!'

PRONUNCIATION GUIDE:

Fionn: *fyun;* **Finnegas:** *finnayguss;* **Conn:** *kon;* **Aillen:** *aylen*

Fionn carefully balanced the salmon on a spit over the fire, poking it with a stick so that it cooked on all sides. But when he started to take the salmon off the spit, he touched the hot skin with his thumb. 'Ouch!' he shouted, and stuck his thumb in his mouth to cool it down.

And then something very strange happened. All at once Fionn felt all the knowledge of the world come rushing into his head.

Finnegas appeared and peered closely at him.

'You look different!' he shouted. 'You have eaten the salmon!'

'I didn't mean to,' said Fionn. 'I burned my thumb and tried to suck it better.'

'Aaaagh! That fish is the Salmon of Wisdom. I've been trying to catch it for years. And now, all the knowledge in it has gone into your thumb!' Finnegas threw the salmon on the ground and began to stamp on it furiously.

Fionn crept quietly away. He took his cloak and travelled towards Tara, where the king lived. He had a plan.

When Fionn came to Tara, he caught his breath in amazement. It was the most wonderful place he had ever seen. An old man, standing at the gates, smiled at Fionn and said: 'You know, in a few days this will be gone. They will have to start building the palace all over again.'

'Why?' asked Fionn.

'Because of the fire-breathing monster that comes every year at Samhain and burns Tara to the ground!'

'Why don't King Conn's soldiers fight him?'

'Why? Because Aillen, the monster, plays the most beautiful music on his harp. As soon as he starts, everyone falls asleep. No one can stay awake to defend Tara.'

'I could stay awake,' said Fionn.

The old man winked at him. 'I just happen to have something that might help you.'

He took up a spear from the ground and handed it to Fionn. The top was covered with a leather bag. Fionn began to pull it off.

'Be careful,' said the old man.

'Uuurgh!' said Fionn.

The old man smiled. 'Yes, it's the most awful smell in the world, isn't it? The tip of the spear has a poison on it.'

'Well,' said Fionn. 'Thank you, I'm sure.' He took the spear and entered the ramparts of Tara.

The king greeted him kindly, but when Fionn asked to be allowed

defend Tara from the monster he frowned.

'You are only a young boy,' the king said. 'The monster will kill you.'

But Fionn begged and begged, and in the end, King Conn agreed.

On Samhain night, everyone left Tara. Everyone but Fionn. Alone on the ramparts, he clutched his new spear in his hand, his heart pounding.

Before long, Fionn saw something coming. A huge, scaly shape was creeping slowly across the moonlit plain, sniffing the ground as it travelled. Blue flames came from its mouth. It came closer and closer.

Then it stopped. The most beautiful music began. The music became a lullaby. Fionn felt his head drop down. His eyes closed. He really, really wanted to sleep. It took all his will power to reach for his spear and drag the leather bag off its tip. Right away, the air filled with the awful smell.

Fionn's eyes sprang open.

The monster stopped playing. His jaw dropped.

'Who are you? And what's that awful smell?' asked the monster.

'I'm Fionn. And *you* are Aillen. I'm here to fight you!'

'We'll see about that!' said Aillen, and blew a flash of flame towards Fionn. But Fionn shook his cloak and put the fire out.

'You are a gifted lad,' the monster said, scratching behind his ear thoughtfully with a long iron claw.

'Well, are you ready to fight?' asked Fionn impatiently.

'Not really, to be honest,' said Aillen. 'I am quite sure that spear wouldn't do me any good if you decided to stick it into me. Can we come to some … arrangement?'

'I will not! Come on, fight! Chicken!'

The monster was still eyeing the spear nervously.

'No need for name-calling. To tell the truth, I'm getting a bit bored doing this every year. I've been thinking of retiring … There's a very good mermaid choir down at Inver Colpa looking for a musician to accompany them. My fiery breath doesn't do any harm in the water.'

'But if I let you go away, you might come back to burn Tara again,' said Fionn.

'I swear I won't. Word of a monster.'

Fionn thought for a minute. The monster batted his blue eyelashes at him. He looked rather like a dog asking for a bone. Fionn made up his mind.

When King Conn arrived back in Tara, everyone was astonished to find the palace still standing. Fionn was waiting on the ramparts, smiling.

'You have killed the monster!' said Conn. 'Tell me what you would like in return.'

Fionn wondered if he should tell Conn that the monster was not really dead. But he had left Aillen practising scales with the mermaids at the mouth of the Boyne. He would not trouble Tara again.

'In return for freeing Tara from the curse of Aillen, I would like to be head of my own group of warriors. I will call them the Fianna!' said Fionn.

'And so it shall be!' said Conn.

And so it was.

In all the stories, it is written that Fionn killed the monster Aillen. Only Fionn and Aillen know better. And now, so do you.

THE BATTLE OF THE HAGS

Muireann lay in bed and watched the dark sky over Loughcrew. The clouds were flying across the moon, making shapes like horses and chariots, dragons and swans, and unicorns with wings. They raced over the smooth green plain and the three round green hills that Muireann could see from her window.

PRONUNCIATION GUIDE:

Muireann: mwirrin

Soon it would be time for the hag to appear. The Loughcrew hag flew over the plain every night. Her white hair streamed behind her, and her eyes were silver. Her black clothes mingled with the tops of the trees. Her face was terrible.

Muireann's parents did not believe her when she told them about the hag and all the other creatures she could see in the clouds.

Tonight, as Muireann gazed at the sky, she noticed that something was different.

Tonight, there were *two* hags.

The little girl sat bolt upright in bed.

One was the usual one. The other was fatter and brighter. She had

a blue face. She looked in the window at Muireann and grinned,

showing gappy teeth. Then she turned to the Loughcrew hag and said:

'Garavogue, do you want to have a contest? And whoever is strongest

will rule this place, as far as the eye can see.'

The Loughcrew hag nodded and said: 'Hag from the South, I've an

idea. Let's see how many rocks we can carry in our aprons. I'll go first.'

Garavogue picked up a pile of rocks, huge rocks, and filled her giant apron with them. Then she flew high into the sky, cackling.

She flew past the houses.

Past the treetops.

Past the hilltops.

Past the clouds.

'I can do better that that,' said the Hag from the South. She picked up dozens of rocks, some even bigger than Garavogue's. She followed the Loughcrew hag up, up into the sky.

Higher and higher went the Hag from the South.

Past the houses.

Past the treetops.

Past the hilltops.

Past the clouds.

Past Garavogue.

Then she went higher than the moon. Finally she stopped.

Far, far below, Muireann looked up. She could see the Hag from the South was struggling to keep hold of her apron full of rocks.

I hope they don't fall and land on me, thought Muireann.

And then the rocks *did* fall!

They fell down past the moon.

Past Garavogue.

Past the clouds.

And they landed with a tremendous CRASH!

Muireann peered out of the window. On top of one of the round green hills was a pile of jagged rocks.

Then there was another CRASH. More rocks fell on top of the second round green hill nearby.

There was a third enormous CRASH, and the last of the rocks flew from the Hag of the South's apron. This time, they fell in the shape of a huge throne.

The Loughcrew hag was shrieking with delight. 'You dropped them! I won! I won! I'm the strongest hag of all,' she called. Then she ran to the throne and sat on it.

The Hag from the South was rubbing her shoulders. 'Well, I'm going home to take a hot bath,' she said. And just like that she was gone.

In the morning, Muireann told her mother and father the story of what had happened while they were all sleeping. Everyone said she must have been dreaming. But no one could explain all the rocks that had appeared on the top of the three green hills overnight. One was in the shape of a throne. You can still go to sit on the Hag's Throne and look over the fields and woods and rivers around Loughcrew. If you are very lucky, you may even see the creatures in the clouds.

HOW AENGUS TRICKED THE DAGDA

Aengus was the son of the Dagda. The Dagda was the king of the Tuatha De Danann, the magical people who ruled Ireland long, long ago. But though his kingdom stretched from Donegal to Kerry, the Dagda would not give Aengus any of his lands or palaces.

Aengus's mother, the Goddess Bóann, said, 'The riverbank of the Boyne is mine. I am going to give you Brú na Bóinne.'

PRONUNCIATION GUIDE:

Aengus: aynghus

But when Aengus came to Brú na Bóinne, the place we now call Newgrange, someone was there before him. It was the Dagda, huge and hairy, snacking on a hambone the size of a small horse.

'Hello, Father,' said Aengus. 'Would you mind handing over my house?'

'I *would* mind,' said the Dagda. 'I like it here. Here I am and here I stay.'

'But this is my house now! Mother said I could have Brú na Bóinne. You are going to have to leave,' said Aengus firmly.

'And who is going to make me?' asked the Dagda.

'I just want to live in my own house,' said Aengus. 'Why won't you leave?'

'Because I am bigger, stronger and older than you,' said the Dagda, picking his teeth with the branch of an oak-tree.

Aengus thought about this for a while. 'Very well,' he said. 'I will give up my claim to the Brú if you let me stay today and tonight. Just from dawn to dusk and from dusk to dawn.'

The Dagda continued picking his teeth, but finally he agreed, 'Just for today and tonight. I want to go hunting anyway. You can mind the house for me, and clean it up while you are at it. It could do with a good tidy-up.'

Early next morning the Dagda returned from the hunt, to find Aengus sitting at the doorway of Brú na Bóinne, smiling.

'You can go away now,' said the Dagda. 'I'm back to take over the place again.'

'I don't think so,' said Aengus. 'You promised to let me have the house for today. It is *today* now, isn't it? And you said I could stay for *tonight* too, remember?'

The Dagda may well have been older, bigger and stronger than his son, but he was not very bright.

'Today, tonight, today,' he muttered. 'I'm confused, but that sounds right.'

Aengus smiled and said, 'Here *I* am and here *I* stay. By the way, I did clean out the house. Your hambone is at the gate. You can pick it up on your way out.'

ART'S QUEST BEYOND THE SEAS

'You cheat!'

There was a sudden silence. Everyone stopped what they were doing and stared. Many of them had seen the invisible hands move Queen Becuma's pieces on the chess board.

Art said furiously, 'You used magic! That's how you won!'

Becuma smiled. 'Conn, your son has lost and must pay a forfeit. Let him go on a quest to find the beautiful Delvcam and bring her to Tara.'

The king loved his only son, but he was completely under the spell of Becuma.

'It might be better if you left Tara for a while, Art,' he said, smiling nervously at his wife.

PRONUNCIATION GUIDE:

Becuma: *baykuma;* **Creide:** *kraydeh*

40

Art kissed his father and left the court. The court went with him to Inver Colpa, the mouth of the Boyne. Everyone knew that Becuma had set him an impossible task. Many of them cried to see him go in his small coracle. But Art didn't cry. He was glad to get away from Becuma. And as he said goodbye to the land of Ireland – so grey and barren – he was not so very sorry to leave it either. Since the day Becuma had been made queen, even the birds had stopped singing.

He began his voyage across the ocean. He had no idea who Delvcam was or where she lived. But Art was brave, and cheerful, and he kept going, further and further into the great ocean. On his journey he was buffeted by storms and freezing winds. Sea monsters rose out of the waves and glared at him with angry eyes. Then one calm day a dolphin swam up beside Art in his coracle and began tugging playfully at his oar.

'You want me to come along with you, then?' asked Art. And the dolphin nodded and smiled his wide dolphin smile.

The dolphin led him to a beautiful island where the fairy woman Creide lived. She wanted to help Art in his quest.

'Head west into the setting sun,' she said. 'There you will find a land full of beauty and danger. But keep going. At the other side of that land you will find an island. That is where Delvcam lives, but she is locked away against her wishes, and you will have to fight for her.'

Art did as Creide said. He finally came to the land far to the west. First he came to an enchanted wood. The trees dropped poison from their branches, but Art used his coracle as an umbrella.

Suddenly there were two hags in front of him, blocking his way. One carried a silver cup and the other a large bath tub.

'You must be thirsty. Have a drink,' the first hag said, offering him the cup.

'No thank you, I'm not thirsty,' said Art. Creide had warned him that the cup was full of poison.

'You must be tired. Rest yourself and have a bath!' said the second hag.

'No thank you, I have had a wash already today,' said Art, for he knew the hag would drown him in a bath of lead.

So the two hags had to let him go on.

The wood ended, and Art arrived at a long, narrow glen. In it lived a thousand giant toads, with tongues full of venom. Art battled his way through them and reached the foot of a high white mountain. He climbed through ice and snow, and more ice and snow, until finally he crossed over the top.

'Perhaps things will be quiet now, for a while!' thought Art hopefully. But he was wrong. At the bottom of the mountain there was a plain full of savage beasts. They roared at him. Art fought them all off with his sword. Then he came to a river, and there was a giant there, guarding the ford. Art overcame him in a fierce battle.

At last, Art reached the seashore and boarded his coracle once again. On an island in the distance was the palace where Delvcam was imprisoned. Around the palace was a fence. On every spike of the fence was a man's head. These were all the brave young princes who had tried to rescue Delvcam.

Art looked into the staring eyes of the murdered princes. How could he succeed where so many had failed?

But then he saw another face, the loveliest he had ever seen. It belonged to Delvcam, and she was smiling at Art.

He called to her: 'Come away with me, Delvcam!'

Delvcam's smile faded. Her mother was a witch and her father was a giant. 'I cannot leave,' she called out to Art. 'My parents will not let me, and they will kill you, just like all the others.'

Before Art could think of a plan, he heard a terrible growl. Behind him was Delvcam's mother! She was terrifying. She was called 'Doghead', and she really did have a dog's head, with vicious teeth and a drooling tongue. Her foul breath poisoned the air around her.

She leapt straight at Art, her jaws aiming for his throat. And so began a long and terrible battle. But finally, Art's sword flashed in the sunlight, and Doghead lay dead, her dog's head sliced from her body by Art's silver sword.

Art was still gasping for breath when he heard another terrible roar.

Morgan, Delvcam's father, was coming towards him! Morgan was a giant, his huge body covered in iron scales. He had claws instead of fingers. His eyes flashed red fire as he spat out the words, 'Time for you to die!'

'Not if I can help it,' said Art, raising his sword. But Art's sword could not pierce the metal scales that covered Morgan.

Within minutes, the monster had brought him to the ground. As the dreadful claws came closer and closer to his neck, Morgan gave a howl of victory. But Art raised his sword and plunged it deep down into the giant's open mouth. Morgan too was dead.

Delvcam came running towards Art, finally freed from her prison. They climbed into the coracle to begin the long journey back to Tara.

When Art and Delvcam reached Ireland, it was greyer and drier and bleaker than ever. But as soon as Delvcam put her foot on the soil, green grass sprang up. Everywhere she went flowers bloomed and birds began to sing. And so they travelled to Tara, leaving a trail of beauty behind them. All along the way people came out of their houses to see them.

'Spring has come back to Ireland with Art and Delvcam!' they cheered.

Conn and Becuma stood waiting for them at the gates of Tara.

Art said: 'Look, Father, I have brought Delvcam home.'

And Delvcam said: 'Now, Ireland will be a happy land again. But Becuma must leave, because she it was who brought misery to Ireland.'

Everyone nodded, even the king. Becuma pulled her green cloak around her and disappeared, never to be seen again. And Art and Delvcam ruled Ireland happily for many, many years.

THE MAGIC BRANCH

❖ ❖ ❖

Once there was a great king, called Cormac. One morning he was out walking on the green grass in front of his palace at Tara. He saw a young man coming towards him, carrying an apple branch. The branch was covered in beautiful apple blossom. The air was filled with the most beautiful scent.

'Why do you come to my kingdom?' the king asked the young man. 'What is it that you wish?'

The young man said nothing, but he shook the apple branch. The blossoms rang out like silver bells. The air was filled with the most beautiful music. It made the king want to dance. It made him want to cry. It made him forget all his troubles. All the sorrow of the world was in the music, and all the laughter too.

He said to the young man: 'That is a wonderful branch. Will you sell it to me?'

The young man smiled. 'It is not for sale. You may have it. But you will have to give me three things in return. Three things that are very dear to you.'

The king thought. What could the young man want? His crown? His lands?

The young man shook the branch again.

Cormac thought then that he could never be happy unless he had the branch. He said to himself: *Even if he takes all the dear things away from me, I will have the branch. Then I will forget my troubles.*

So he nodded. The young man looked at the king and raised one eyebrow. He handed him the branch. Then he said: 'I will be back in a year for the first dear thing.'

A year to the day, the young man arrived back in Cormac's court at Tara. He took away Cormac's daughter. Cormac cried. So did all his people. But when the king shook the magic branch, everyone forgot how sad they were, for a while.

The next year the stranger came again. This time he took away Cormac's son. Everyone cried. But the king shook the magic branch and, once again, everyone forgot how sad they were.

Then, after the third year, the stranger came to take away Cormac's wife.

Each year Cormac had been getting sadder and sadder. You cannot listen to even the most beautiful music all the time. And now, when he shook the branch, even its magic made him sad.

So when the young man led his wife away, Cormac went too. He followed the stranger for mile after mile. He walked and walked, over the horizon, on a path made of sunset. His feet became sore. His shoes wore out. His fine clothes were torn on brambles and did not keep the rain or the cold out any more. One wild day, his crown was carried away by the west wind.

I am as poor as any beggar, thought Cormac. *Poorer, because I have no family. I gave them away. I am the stupidest man in the world.*

But he kept going, following the stranger and his wife. And one day the three travellers reached the seashore. The stranger mounted one of the white horses that pranced in from the ocean. He pulled Cormac's wife up behind him. Cormac jumped onto another white horse and followed them into the depths of the ocean. Down into the waves they went.

I don't care if I drown, thought Cormac. *Perhaps in another life I will meet my family once more.*

But he did not drown. In fact, the Land Beneath the Waves was a wonderful place. Mermaids smiled at him as they swam past him, combing their long green and blue hair. Golden sand glittered at his feet. All around him were strange-looking fish and waving plants of the most amazing colours. And everything was silent, with the silence of the deep sea.

And then Cormac came to a palace thatched with white seagulls'
feathers. Cormac knew he had come to the realm of King Manannán
Mac Lir, King of the Sea.

He went into the seagull palace. All at once, his ears were filled with
the most beautiful music. Cormac realised that the figure on the throne
was the same young man who had taken his family away. Here he was
a great king, wearing a crown of gold and silver fishes. He smiled at
Cormac, and Cormac bowed low; because while Cormac was the High
King of Ireland, this was the king of all the wide oceans.

'Why do you come to my kingdom?' Manannán asked.

'I come to beg a great favour,' said Cormac. 'I have learned to value what I have lost. Please give me back my children and my wife. And in return I will give you back your magic branch.'

Manannán smiled. 'You have learned well. Your wife and son and daughter may return with you to Tara. And you may keep the Branch of Sweetness. I wish to give you another gift. This is the Cup of Truth. If three lies are told, it will break to pieces. If three true things are said, it will be made whole again.'

Cormac bowed low. When he looked up, three figures were coming towards him, out of the blue shadows behind the king. He rushed forward and hugged his wife and children for a long, long time.

Next morning, when he woke, he was back in Tara. His family was there with him. Beside him was the Cup of Truth and the Branch of Sweetness.

Cormac became the wisest king Ireland had ever known, and his reign the happiest ever. And they say, that when the cows in the fields lie down on a summer's evening and sigh, it is because they are remembering the happy time when King Cormac ruled over Ireland.

First published 2016 by The O'Brien Press Ltd,
12 Terenure Road East, Rathgar, Dublin 6, D06 HD27, Ireland.
Tel: +353 1 4923333; Fax: +353 1 4922777
E-mail: books@obrien.ie
Website: www.obrien.ie
The O'Brien Press is a member of Publishing Ireland.

ISBN: 978-1-84717-683-7

6 5 4 3 2 1
20 19 18 17 16

Printed and bound in the Czech Republic by Finidr Ltd.
The paper in this book is produced using pulp from managed forests.

NEWGRANGE, TARA AND THE BOYNE VALLEY

HIGH CROSSES, KELLS

LOUGHCREW
CAIRNS

KELLS

OLD
MELLIFONT
ABBEY

LOUGHCREW CAIRNS

NAVAN

TRIM CASTLE

TRIM CASTLE